NO PLACE
LIKE SPACE

For the aliens who crash-landed into my life: Larry, Ashley, and Austin—L.H.

For Ben, an inspiring brother who's always looking up—J.W.

Text copyright © 2017 by Lisa Harkrader
Illustrations copyright © 2017 by Jessica Warrick
Galaxy Scout Activities illustrations copyright © 2017 by Kane Press, Inc.
Galaxy Scout Activities illustrations by Nadia DiMattia

Library of Congress Cataloging-in-Publication Data

Names: Harkrader, Lisa. | Warrick, Jessica, illustrator.
Title: No place like space / by Lisa Harkrader ; illustrated by Jessica Warrick.
Description: New York : The Kane Press, 2017. | Series: How to be an earthling ; 5
Identifiers: LCCN 2016023683 (print) | LCCN 2016043054 (ebook) |
ISBN 9781575658476 (pbk) | ISBN 9781575658438 (reinforced library binding) |
ISBN 9781575658513 (ebook)
Subjects: | CYAC: Extraterrestrial beings—Fiction. | Schools—Fiction. |
Homesickness—Fiction. | Humorous stories.
Classification: LCC PZ7.H22615 Nip 2017 (print) | LCC PZ7.H22615 (ebook) |
DDC [Fic]—dc23
LC record available at https://lccn.loc.gov/2016023683

1 3 5 7 9 10 8 6 4 2

First published in the United States of America in 2017 by Kane Press, Inc.
Printed in China

Book Design: Edward Miller

How to Be an Earthling is a registered trademark of Kane Press, Inc.

Visit us online at **www.kanepress.com**

 Like us on Facebook
facebook.com/kanepress

 Follow us on Twitter
@KanePress

CONTENTS

***Don't miss a single one
of Spork's adventures!***

NO PLACE
LIKE SPACE

by Lisa Harkrader
illustrated by Jessica Warrick

KANE PRESS
New York

Spork

Trixie Lopez

Mrs. Buckle

Jack Donnelly

Piper Cho

Grace Hanford

Adam Novak

Newton Miller

Jo Jo

REPORT TO TROOP

BEEP. BEEP. BEEEEEEEEP!
Greetings, Galaxy Scouts! I've found something that will earn me a Solo Explorer badge for sure.

It might even make up for some of my past messes. You may not have noticed, but I've crashed into some things.

That's one confusing thing about Earthlings. They do everything they can to crash—and then try not to. They put wheels on their shoes and try not to crash. They put wheels on planks, stand on them, and try not to crash. I've even seen Earthlings try to ride on one wheel. Then try not to crash.

But I've found something—or someone—who will give me the wisdom to understand all that. I'll have so much wisdom, I'll never crash again. I'm sure of it.

Pretty sure.

Almost completely sure.

1

GNOME AWAY FROM HOME

Trixie scurried through the hall, her book bag bouncing on her back. She swerved around the janitor. She dodged a clump of kindergartners. She breezed past the art room, sending the paper butterflies on the bulletin board fluttering.

Today the third grade was planning the best event of the whole school year. Trixie couldn't wait.

As she rounded a corner, Spork darted past. He was cradling something in his arms.

"Hi, Spork!" Trixie said. "Guess what today—"

Spork didn't slow down. He reached their classroom and skittered inside.

Trixie frowned. Spork always said hi. She shrugged. He was probably excited to get to class, too.

Spork was a space alien. His flying saucer had crash-landed on the school playground. Now he was officially a third grader.

Inside the classroom, Trixie found the rest of the class—including their teacher, Mrs. Buckle—gathered around Spork's desk. Trixie squeezed between her two best friends, Grace and Newton, to see what was so interesting.

Spork had placed a little ceramic man on his desk. It had boots and a beard and a pointy red hat. Spork's antennae quivered in awe as he gazed at the little man.

Jack snorted. "Is that a garden gnome?"

"A *garden* gnome." Spork's eyes filled with wonder. "He must be. I found him in the school garden."

"Spork," said Mrs. Buckle in her most understanding teacher voice, "the gnome was in the garden because I put it there. I saw it at a garage sale and thought it would make a nice ornament. It's called a garden gnome for a reason. It's supposed to stay in the garden."

"Oh, he won't stay," said Spork. "Gnomes travel to unexpected places. They bring wisdom home from the far reaches of the universe. They're honored elders on my planet." He sighed. "And today, I've finally met one."

CLOSED MOUTH: THE BEST WAY TO KEEP SECRETS

TALL HAT TO HOLD EXTRA WISDOM

WEATHERPROOF BEARD TO WARM THE NECK

MAGIC PANTS-RETAINING BELT

STURDY BOOTS FOR LONG TRIPS

Trixie studied the little man. He wasn't doing much—just standing there like any regular-old, ordinary garden gnome.

"Are you sure this is the same kind of gnome?" she asked.

"The wisest elders neither speak nor move," said Spork. "They watch and wait . . . and listen. They communicate in ancient, mysterious ways. No one knows exactly how."

The bell rang.

Spork covered the gnome's ears.

"Never fear," Spork told him. "That's only a schedule notification device. It tells Earthlings when to do things. It's noisy, but it's not dangerous." Spork's eyes grew wide. "That's a piece of wisdom you can take home to our planet. And I helped you find it."

Spork pulled a notebook from his desk and scribbled something in it.

Mrs. Buckle smiled. "I can see you've become attached to the little guy, Spork. You can keep him on your desk for now. But he'll have to go back to the garden at some point."

Spork nodded. "He'll know when it's time."

"I'm sure he will." Mrs. Buckle clapped her hands. "Now let's find our seats. I have an announcement."

Finally! Trixie scrambled to her desk.

"Today we start planning the school carnival," said Mrs. Buckle. "As you know, each grade is in charge of something. This year, the third grade gets to choose the carnival theme."

The theme? Trixie could hardly

believe it. This was better than she'd hoped for.

Spork raised his hand. "This carnival. Is it a place to find wisdom?"

Trixie didn't wait for Mrs. Buckle to answer. "It's a place to find *fun*," she said. "Last year we had bowling and a ring toss and face painting. I came in first in the free-throw contest and won a stuffed lion."

Spork swallowed. "It sounds like Blast Fest." His voice was quiet. "Galaxy Scouts looked forward to it every year. We had games, contests, prizes . . . and rides."

"Exactly like the carnival!" said Trixie. "I'll bet Blast Fest was, well—"

"A blast?" said Jack.

"It was." Spork pulled the gnome closer. A sad look washed over his face. "It was a real"—he gulped—"blast."

Trixie's heart fluttered. First the garden gnome. Now Blast Fest. Was Spork getting . . . homesick?

2

IF THE
BOOT FITS

"Pirates!"

"Mermaids!

Chattering voices pulled Trixie from her thoughts. Third grade was planning the carnival without her!

Trixie waved her hand. "I know! We could do—"

"The Wild West!" said Newton. "We could play horseshoes."

"Or," said Trixie, "we could—"

"Have a square dance," said Grace.

"A square dance?" Jack snorted. "Great idea—if we don't want anyone to come. Why don't we do something fun? Like a haunted house, with bats and skeletons—and ghosts."

"Ghosts?" Newton's face went pale.

Jack laughed. "You're not afraid, are you?"

Newton swallowed.

"Of course he's not," said Grace. "But the carnival is for the whole school. I'm sure Newton thinks a haunted house might be too scary for younger kids."

Newton gave Grace a grateful look.

Jack rolled his eyes. "We can't let scared little babies ruin our fun."

"We do want to have fun," said Mrs. Buckle. "But we also need to show kindness."

"Kindness?" Spork blinked. "Is that Earth wisdom?"

"In a way." Mrs. Buckle smiled. "Kindness means caring about other people. And it means when you see people in need or sad—or scared—you put yourself in their shoes. You try to help them."

"Shoes." Spork nodded. "*More* wisdom to take home." He wrote something in his notebook.

"I'm glad we're talking about kindness," said Mrs. Buckle. "We have a

busy couple of weeks coming up. We're going to need to be kind to each other. I challenge all of you to be as kind as possible and see what happens."

The class spent all morning trying to be kind—and trying to pick a theme.

"Fairy tales," said one kid.

"Beach party," said someone else.

Trixie frowned. Beach balls were fun. But they weren't kind.

"I know!" said Trixie. "Puppies!"

"Puppies?" said Jack. "That's not a theme."

Trixie slumped in her chair. Puppies were way more kind than beach balls.

As she sat there,

Trixie felt something tug at her foot.
She looked down. Spork was crouched
by her desk, pulling off her boot.

"Spork!" she said.

Mrs. Buckle came over to see what
was going on. "Uh, Spork. What are
you doing?"

Spork slid Trixie's boot onto his own
foot. "Putting myself in Trixie's shoe."

He wiggled his foot. "You were right. I feel sturdy. Ready to march."

Mrs. Buckle smiled. "Putting yourself in someone's shoes is just a saying, Spork. It means you try to understand how another person is feeling."

Spork frowned. "You don't do that with shoes?"

Mrs. Buckle shook her head. "You do it with your heart."

Spork slid Trixie's boot off and handed it back to her. He plodded over to his desk and erased something in his notebook.

"Kindness is very confusing," he said. "I really think shoes would help."

Finally it was time for lunch. As they left the classroom, Grace held the door.

"That's very kind," Mrs. Buckle told her.

When they went through the lunch line, Spork was juggling the gnome in one hand and his notebook in the other. So Newton carried his tray.

"Newton is showing kindness," Spork told the gnome.

Trixie sighed. Sure, Grace and Newton were kind. They were almost famous for it. But Trixie could be kind. She could be very kind. She could be the kindest kid in the whole third grade.

And she would prove it.

3

THE
TROUBLE WITH
KINDNESS

Trixie spent lunch period looking for someone to be kind to.

She watched Newton scoop up his last bit of applesauce.

"Aha!" said Trixie.

She snatched his tray and darted
to the dump bins at the back of the
lunchroom.

"Hey!" Newton hollered through a
mouthful of applesauce.

"No need to thank me," Trixie called.
She scraped Newton's tray and stacked
it with the others.

She turned to find Newton behind
her, watching in horror.

"I wasn't finished," he said.

Trixie swallowed. "You weren't?"

Newton shook his head and trudged back to their table.

Trixie followed. "I'm sorry," she said. "I was showing kindness."

"That's okay." Newton sighed. "But next time don't dump my tater tots. I was saving them for last."

"You can share mine," said Grace.

"That's *really* kind," said Newton.

Spork watched Newton pop a tot into his mouth. "Kindness seems to include processed potato morsels," Spork told the gnome.

KINDNESS =

"Processed potato morsels are the best part of kindness," said Newton.

Trixie sighed. Kindness! It was easy for Grace and Newton. Trixie tried it and only made things worse.

Spork had finished eating. Now he was gazing into the gnome's eyes. Waiting for wisdom, Trixie thought.

Her heart fluttered. Spork was homesick. What he needed was . . . something from home!

Trixie gave a triumphant smile. "I have the perfect carnival theme," she told her friends. "Blast Fest."

Grace's eyes grew wide.

Newton blinked behind his glasses. "An outer space theme," he said.

"That *is* perfect." Grace slapped Trixie a high-five.

Even Jack gave a reluctant nod. "Not bad."

The third grade all started talking at once. All except Spork. Trixie thought he'd thank her. Instead, he just stared with his mouth open.

Trixie nudged him. "Are you okay?" she whispered.

"Okay?" Spork swallowed. "You bet."
"I am a-okay, one hundred percent,
hunky-dunky, all systems go."

Trixie nodded. But she couldn't help
frowning. No matter how many ways
he said it, Spork didn't *seem* okay.

When the kids got back to class, they
told Mrs. Buckle the theme.

"I love it," she said. "Let's get to work
planning the carnival."

theme:
OUTER SPACE!

As the class came up with ideas, Mrs. Buckle wrote them on the board.

"We'll have a Moonwalk," said one kid.

"And Flying Saucers," said another. "With Frisbees."

"We could use the gym scooters and have a scooter race," said Jack. "We'll call it—"

"Rocket Launch!" said Newton.

"We need snacks," said Jack. "How about—"

"Jelly!" said Grace. "We'll call it Gloop. And have peanut butter and  'Gloop' sandwiches."

Trixie glanced at Spork. Every time someone called out an idea, Spork slumped lower in his chair. Trixie's heart fluttered again. She thought giving him something from home would help. But was Blast Fest making him even more homesick?

Beside her, Jack slumped, too. Trixie knew why. Every time Jack came up with an idea, somebody else came up with something better. He sat at his desk, his head down.

Trixie's heart gave another flutter. She frowned. A flutter . . . for Jack? It didn't make sense. Jack never showed kindness toward anybody. But now he was hurting. And she couldn't help it. She wanted to be kind.

Trixie shook her head. This kindness thing was complicated. Now she'd have to be kind to Jack while trying to think up another way to be kind to Spork. It would be easier if she could be kind to both of them at once.

That was it! She'd ask Jack to help her come up with an idea for Spork. By helping Jack, she'd get his help in helping Spork. It was a kindness two-fer!

She leaned toward Jack. "We need to come up with an idea."

Jack cut his eyes toward her. "We? Why me?"

Trixie shrugged. "You have great ideas. And right now we need an idea so great, it'll help Spork feel less homesick. An idea so big, everyone will notice. An idea so kind, Mrs. Buckle will probably give us a prize for kindness."

"A prize." Jack nodded. "I'm in."

4

SPORK'S CRASH LANDING

Trixie stood at the edge of the playground. She and Jack had come up with the most amazing—and *kind*—surprise for Spork. They'd worked for weeks getting it ready.

The whole school had helped with

the carnival. Now the banners were up and the games were in place. Mrs. Buckle was patrolling the rides. Grace, Newton, and Jack were lined up with Trixie, waiting for the fun to begin.

But where was Spork?

Trixie finally spotted him threading his way through the carnival booths. He was clutching the gnome and had his notebook jammed into his pocket.

Trixie darted over and grabbed his hand. "Come on," she said. "We don't want to miss anything."

"Oh, I don't miss things," said Spork

as he skittered along behind her. "Even when I try."

First they rode Rocket Launch. Trixie, Jack, Grace, Newton, and Spork sat cross-legged on their scooters at the starting line. Mrs. Buckle blew the whistle. Trixie pushed off. She shot past Grace, then Newton. But Jack was fast. Trixie and Jack scooted down the lane, neck and neck. They crossed the finish line in a tie.

Trixie gave Jack a fist bump. "Good race!"

She looked back. Spork was still creeping along, inch by inch. He and the gnome had barely made it past the starting line.

Next they tried the Moonwalk. Spork stared at the bounce house.

"I've walked on a moon before," he said. "On several, in fact. Real moons aren't much fun."

"This one's different," said Trixie.

Trixie climbed into the Moonwalk. Then she turned and pulled Spork up after her. Their friends scrambled in behind them.

Trixie bounced and flipped, first standing up, then

sitting down. She bounced into Grace
and then into Newton, who bounced
into Jack. They all fell down laughing.

"What do you think?" Trixie asked Spork.

"It *is* different," he said. "Real moons aren't this soft. And they don't have nice, safe walls to hold you in. Moons could really use some walls. The low gravity makes it hard to stay put."

Spork did a couple of nice safe bounces. Then he sat very still with the gnome and tried not to tip over.

Finally Trixie and Jack led Spork to their big surprise. It was a giant inflatable slide. A big pool of balls lay at the bottom. A huge sheet was draped over the top.

Trixie leaned toward Jack. "This will be the kindest ride for sure."

Grace gave Trixie a funny look.

"Kindness isn't a competition," she said.

Before Trixie could say anything, Mrs. Buckle clapped her hands.

"Everyone ready?" she asked.

Trixie grabbed one side of the sheet. Jack grabbed the other. Mrs. Buckle counted to three, and they pulled it away. Underneath was a sign:

SPORK'S CRASH LANDING

"What do you think?" Trixie asked Spork. "Does it remind you of home?"

Spork stared at the sign. "You have no idea," he said.

Trixie and her friends lined up at the steps. Trixie pulled Spork into line next to her.

"Ready . . . GO!" said
Mrs. Buckle.

Spork swallowed. "Are you
sure—?"

"Come on!" Trixie grabbed
Spork's arm.

They raced up the back of the slide.
They reached the top, scrambled over—

and plummeted down the other side. As
they rocketed toward the bottom, Spork
and the gnome bounced off one side of
the slide, then the other.

"Oh, no!" cried Spork. "We're
going to craaaaa—"

They plunged into the ball
pool at the bottom. Balls
exploded all over the
playground.

Trixie laughed and gasped for breath.

"That was amazing!" said Grace.

"Excellent!" Newton straightened his glasses.

Jack slapped Trixie a high-five. "Sweet!"

Trixie turned to Spork. He sat in the middle of the mess of balls, a horrified look on his face.

"I ruined Blast Fest," he whispered. "Again."

5

THE GNOME KNOWS

"What do you mean, *again*?" said Trixie.

Spork hung his head. "The last time Galaxy Scouts held Blast Fest, I—I crashed. I lost one of our best rocket racers down a meteor crater. I dented the Scout space station. I caused so much damage, they had to cancel Blast Fest the next year. They haven't had one since." He swallowed. "Now I've wrecked the carnival, too. It's what I was afraid of."

"*That's* what you've been worried about?" said Trixie. "Wrecking the carnival?"

"You didn't wreck it," said Grace.

"Yeah. These are a bunch of plastic balls. You're *supposed* to crash into them." Jack picked up one of the balls and bounced it off his head. "See? You didn't wreck anything."

"What about this?" Spork pulled the gnome from behind his back. It was in two pieces. The gnome's head had snapped off in the crash.

"Oh, no!" said Grace.

"Not the gnome!" said Newton.

Trixie's heart fluttered. Spork looked
so sad.

Mrs. Buckle examined the two
pieces.

"Pottery isn't hard to fix," she said.
"A little glue should do it."

"Or a little Gloop," said Trixie.

"Pottery . . ." Spork's antennae drooped. "You were right, Mrs. Buckle. He isn't the kind of gnome I thought he was."

"Maybe not," said Mrs. Buckle. "Maybe when the real gnomes visited, they were so wise that Earthlings made little statues of them."

Spork looked up. "Do you think so?"

"And he can still be a good garden gnome," said Grace.

Trixie studied the gnome pieces in Spork's hand. "What's that?" she asked.

Spork frowned. He reached into the gnome and pulled out a piece of paper. He unfolded it and started to read. His eyes grew wide. He held the paper so everyone could see.

Honored Gnome Traveler:

Congratulations! You have successfully located the Top Secret Wisdom Deposit Station for this district. Carefully place any wisdom you have discovered inside the base of this station. We will collect and catalog it for the benefit of future generations. Thank you for your worthy service.

The Elder Council

"You know what this means?" Trixie asked. "You found the secret way gnomes communicate! Your garden gnome is like a mailbox for the real gnomes."

Spork blinked. "You know what else it means?" He tugged his notebook from his pocket. "I've been gathering wisdom for my gnome. *He* can't take it, but the real gnomes can. I'll deposit it inside so they can collect it."

He started tearing out the sheets of wisdom from his notebook.

He stopped. He put his hand on Trixie's arm.

"Thank you," he said. "If it weren't for Spork's Crash Landing, I never would've discovered this."

Trixie grinned. She wanted to say, "You're welcome." She wanted to tell Spork how she and Jack had convinced the principal to get the slide and how they made the sign and hid it under the sheet early that morning before anyone else arrived. She wanted Spork to see how kind she was. She wanted *everyone* to see how kind she was.

Then she noticed Jack standing beside the ball pool, his head down.

"Don't thank me," Trixie said. "It was Jack's idea."

Jack looked up in surprise.

"Thank you, Jack," said Spork.

He held up his hand. Jack gave him a high-five.

Mrs. Buckle put her arm around Trixie's shoulder. "I saw what you did there." She gave Trixie a wink. "That was one of the kindest things I've seen in quite a while."

"Maybe." Trixie smiled. "But kindness isn't a competition."

REPORT TO TROOP

BEEP. BEEP. BEEP.

Um, about that discovery? The one that would earn me a new badge?

Well, it would . . . except I can't tell you about it. It's an ancient secret. I think it's supposed to stay that way.

Here's a discovery I can tell you about: Crashing can be fun—if you have something soft to crash into. I kept crashing into hard things, like asteroids and playgrounds.

Earthlings are very kind about crashing. They even give trophies for it. I won Best Crash Ever.

That's another thing I discovered: kindness. Sometimes kindness is about shoes. Once in a while it's about potatoes. But mostly it's about hearts. It's understanding what's in someone else's heart. It's feeling in your own heart that you want to help.

Crashing plus kindness plus trophies. This Earth place was made for me!

GALAXY SCOUTS

ACTIVITIES

Greetings!

I am getting so Earth-wise! Mrs. Buckle told me to put myself in someone else's shoes. But not their actual shoes. Or boots. Or flip-flops. (Even though I love flip-flops. Earthling footwear is amazing!) But now I know Mrs. Buckle meant we have to imagine how other people feel and be as kind to them as we want them to be to us. Take this quiz to find out if you're just kind of kind or a Kindness Superstar!

—Spork

(There can be more than one right answer.)

1. Your friend hurt her ankle playing Meteor Toss at the Galaxy Fair. How could you show her kindness?
   a. Go to the Nurse Nebula to get her help.
   b. Throw some Gloop at her and hope for the best.
   c. Tell her about the time you hurt your foot playing Supernova Surf.
   d. Help her to a seat so she can put her leg up.

2. Your friend lost her glasses on the Venus Voyage ride. What would you do?
   a. Yell, "Somebody help her find her glasses!"
   b. Go back to Venus Voyage and look for them.
   c. Ask, "How many fingers am I holding up?"
   d. Check the Lost and Found to see if anyone turned in glasses.

3. Nerp is sad because he wanted to go on the Lunar Loop-de-Loop, but Dwyz won't go with him. So you:

    a. Say Dwyz is just a scaredy-flarg for not going on the Loop-de-Loop.

    b. Tell Nerp that the Loop-de-Loop is lame.

    c. Offer to go on the Loop-de-Loop with Nerp.

    d. Ask Nerp to play Rocket Race with you instead.

4. Your friend came in last in the Rocket Race. You:

    a. Encourage him to try again and see if he can do any better.

    b. Tell him you came in first!

    c. Give him advice on how to be quicker.

    d. Remind him it's just a game. Having fun is what matters.

Answers:

1. *A* and *d* are both great answers. She is hurting and maybe even a little embarrassed, so bringing her to a safe spot and getting her help would be ways to show kindness. (And those Nebulous Nurses are whizzes at fixing meteor injuries!)

2. Helping your friend find her lost glasses is the kind thing to do, so *b* and *d* would be good answers because Venus Voyage and the Lost and Found would both be good places to check. (Trust me, Galactic Lost and Found Officers can find *anything*.)

3. Name calling is never kind, so *a* is not the way to go. *C* would be very kind—or if you don't like the Loop-de-Loop either, suggest something else, like in answer *d!*

4. Bragging about your achievements when someone else is feeling bad isn't kind, so cross out *b*. You can try *c*, but it's a good idea to ask someone if they want advice before just giving it. *A* and *d*, encouraging him to try again and just have fun, are the kindest things you can do.

Rocket Launch

My Earth friends Grace, Jack, Trixie, and Newton decided to have a rematch of their scooter race. They asked me to declare the winner, but when they crossed the finish line, something in the sky distracted me. I thought it was a space pod, but it was just a really overfed pigeon.

When I asked who won the race, they all gave me different information. I was so confused! Can you figure out which place each of my friends came in?

- Trixie said, "I beat Newton."
- Newton said, "I was slower than Jack."
- Grace said, "I was faster than everyone but Trixie."
- Jack said, "I came in third."

Answer: Trixie came in first place, Grace came in second, Jack came in third, and Newton came in fourth.

Space Riddle

Here's my favorite space riddle! Only two of us in my Galaxy Scout troop could solve it. Can you?

"I am the beginning of the end, the end of every place. I am the beginning of eternity, the end of time and space. What am I?"

Answer: The letter e.

MEET THE AUTHOR AND ILLUSTRATOR

LISA HARKRADER lives and writes in a small town in Kansas. She tries to act like a proper Earthling, but usually feels more like an alien.

JESSICA WARRICK has illustrated lots of picture books about dogs, cats, and kids, but she is mostly interested in drawing aliens, for some strange reason. She does a pretty good job acting like an Earthling . . . most of the time.

Spork just landed on Earth, and look, he already has lots of fans!

★ **Moonbeam Children's Book Awards Gold Medal**
Best Book Series—Chapter Books

★ **Moonbeam Children's Book Awards Silver Medal**
Juvenile Fiction—Early Reader/Chapter Books
for book #1 *Spork Out of Orbit*

"Young readers are going to love this series! Spork is a funny and unexpected main character. Kids will love his antics and sweet disposition. Teachers and parents will appreciate the subtle messages embedded in the stories. The kids in the stories genuinely like each other, which I found refreshing. I will be giving these books to my young friends."—**Ron Roy**, author of A to Z Mysteries, Calendar Mysteries, and Capital Mysteries

"A breezy, humorous lesson in honesty that never stoops to didacticism. The other three volumes publishing simultaneously address similarly weighty lessons—lying, shyness, bullying, and responsibility—all with a multicultural cast of Everykids. . . . A good choice for those new to chapters."
—**Kirkus** for book #1 *Spork Out of Orbit*

"This is a book where readers, kids, and aliens learn together, experiencing how words and choices affect all of us. It's simple, elegant, and very insightful storytelling. *Greetings, Sharkling!* doesn't waste a single page of opportunity."
—**The San Francisco Book Review**

"I'm so glad Spork landed on Earth! His misadventures are playful and sweet, and I love the clever wordplay!"
—**Becca Zerkin**, former children's book reviewer for the *New York Times Book Review* and *School Library Journal*

"Kids will love reading about Spork. Parents, teachers, and librarians will love reading aloud this series to those same kids."—**Rob Reid**, author of *Silly Books to Read Aloud*

How to Be an Earthling
Winner of the Moonbeam Gold Medal
for Best Chapter Book Series!

Respect

Honesty

Responsibility

Courage

Kindness

Perseverance

Citizenship

Self-Control

To learn more about Spork, go to kanepress.com

Check out these other series from Kane Press

Animal Antics A to Z®
(Grades PreK–2 • Ages 3–8)
Winner of two *Learning* Magazine Teachers' Choice Awards
"A great product for any class learning about letters!"
—*Teachers' Choice Award reviewer comment*

Let's Read Together®
(Grades PreK–3 • Ages 4–8)
"Storylines are silly and inventive, and recall Dr. Seuss's *Cat in the Hat*
for the building of rhythm and rhyming words."—*School Library Journal*

Holidays & Heroes
(Grades 1–4 • Ages 6–10)
"Commemorates the influential figures behind important American
celebrations. This volume emphasizes the importance of lofty ambitions
and fortitude in the face of adversity…"—*Booklist* (for *Let's Celebrate Martin
Luther King Jr. Day*)

Math Matters®
(Grades K–3 • Ages 5–8)
Winner of a *Learning* Magazine Teachers' Choice Award
"These cheerfully illustrated titles offer primary-grade
children practice in math as well as reading."—*Booklist*

The Milo & Jazz Mysteries®
(Grades 2–5 • Ages 7–11)
"Gets it just right."—*Booklist,* starred review (for *The Case
of the Stinky Socks*); *Book Links'* Best New Books for the Classroom

Mouse Math®
(Grades PreK & up • Ages 4 & up)
"The Mouse Math series is a great way to integrate math and literacy into
your early childhood curriculum. My students thoroughly enjoyed these
books."—*Teaching Children Mathematics*

Science Solves It!®
(Grades K–3 • Ages 5–8)
"The Science Solves It! series is a wonderful tool for
the elementary teacher who wants to integrate reading
and science."—*National Science Teachers Association*

Social Studies Connects®
(Grades K–3 • Ages 5–8)
"This series is very strongly recommended…."—*Children's Bookwatch*
"Well done!"—*School Library Journal*

KANEPRESS.com